Will His Kingdom Come?

By

Robert Paul & Luby M.

INTRODUCTION

Wow! 25 years in ministry and has nothing to show for it. Where has he gone wrong? Kingdom asked himself. Anyways, it is bad it took him this long to realize he was moving around and not going anywhere. This book, Will His Kingdom Come?, narrates the life of a young man (Kingdom) from his childhood to when he began working as a pastor. This book has a touch of the Anioma culture and few words typical of the Nigerian society.

Now let us go back to how it all started.

Just like every other African child Kingdom was brought up in a quiet village, Umauja in ukwuani local government area, Delta State. His parents were farmers. His father who sometimes indulged in menial activities just to put food on the table considered himself a hardworking man. Yes in his days he was a gold miner. He worked for a few people for years before retiring home to join his wife fully in the farm work. Kingdom had siblings, Kento, Adakwu, Blessing, Morris the last born, and less I forget Becca his half-sister. Kingdom's father Aquilla had an affair with a woman and Becca was the end product of that affair. Becca was born shortly after Kingdom was born. This infuriated his wife Berna but there was nothing she could do, the deed has already been done. Berna and her husband trained their children to do their very best, but you know African children, grow up to walk in their paths. Berna loved her children and showed more love to her first daughter Ada, Becca was the outcast of the family, no matter how hard she tried to impress the family, Berna hated her. Becca had nowhere to go since her mother died when she was only nine. Her father tried all his best to make sure she never felt out of place, but as a man, he wasn't always at home, Berna made life miserable for poor Becca. Kingdom paid no attention to what happened in his home, his main goal was to live better than his parents.

CHAPTER ONE

The early days

At twelve Kingdom became a hunter, and he would go hunting with his father. At that young age, the southpaw had dexterity in many things plus his doggedness. Being the first son Kingdom understood the need to be strong emotionally. Although he was strong physically and emotionally Kento was up the chart. Kento had the spirit of a good judge combined with wisdom and calmness. But physically he was a mummy's boy who had little or no strength to fight his peers.

Kingdom in his stout stature was always seen as the wisest among his peers, yes he was wise and cunning just like the tortoise, and they called him tortoise sometimes.

One day, the weather was very friendly to hunters so Kingdom and his friends, Ofor, Okei, Jude, Moses and

Akalaka the weakling of the group decided to go for their usual hunting. Hunting was something they loved doing. Kingdom saw Kento his brother as a small boy so he never liked dragging his babyish as along to hunt. He felt his brother belonged in the kitchen with their mother since he always loved cuddling close to their mother.

On that fateful day just, as usual, he left home with his friends into the bush. He promised his mother a huge rabbit so she can use it in making dinner later. Berna knew what she was expecting and her son never failed. Of course, her son learned from the best. The smile on her face was contagious. The bush welcomed them with its usual quietness. The six sang along with joy in their heart, they looked like men who just won a battle. But has the battle started? No!!! Okei (meaning the old one) had the face of a warrior, he hardly smiled. He was named Okei because his parents believed he was the reincarnation of his grandfather. He led the group in courageous songs. Songs he learned from his father. Far gone into the bush they sighted a very well position hole believed to be that of a rabbit.

Kingdom in his authoritative tone asked them not to dig it yet and reserve it for the last. It looked big and it should be the last to be dug. They found other small holes, dug and caught many rabbits enough for the days demand. They were satisfied. Now it was time to dig the mighty hole with the big rabbit. Kingdom and his friends began digging. When they were satisfied with how deep they dug, Akalaka the weakling was asked to put his hands to feel the rabbit inside, he wasn't just a weakling he was considered an idiot too who couldn't tell his right and left. Akalaka did as instructed and told them the rabbit's body was very smooth. For suggested it was an old rabbit who no longer had furs.

They continued digging lo and behold they dug up a big hungry python, bigger than any snake they had ever seen in their life. An agitated python, they dare destroy its home. It immediately charged toward them it was too late to fight they ran for their dear lives. Even the almighty Kingdom did not wait to fight. They ran and left their rabbits. They not only disturbed the python, but they also brought food for it, what consolation. The python ate the rabbits to its fill and crept back to its remaining abode. Meanwhile, the boys were still running stumbling upon each other. After running for about 30 minutes, Moses remembered their rabbits and cried, begging them to go back but none of them was willing to embark on that dangerous journey. All of a sudden they stopped running, panting; now it dawned on them that they left their games behind.

Kingdom urged them to go back and said anyone who refuses to go back with them was not a man. Deep down Kingdom was scared but he dare not show it he loses his respect for his colleagues. They reluctantly agreed to go back, the same distance took them almost an hour to arrive. Unfortunately, their day's game was gone. For the first time, Kingdom broke down in tears before his friends. He cried because his mother was waiting for him. That day's dinner depended on him. He had hoped to sell some of his shares and his mother would buy foodstuff with the proceeds. Then the remaining part of his share will serve as meat for the soup. His friends joined in the outpouring of tears. They all came from poor homes and they each supported their homes in one way or the other. The six friends left for the village with heavy hearts and had nothing to present to their families. They couldn't summon up the courage to go to their houses, instead, they sat under the famous udala tree at the village square sulking at their failure. Past 9 they were not still home. Mama Kingdom became worried. Mama Okei and Mama Ofor came to Berna's house only to find out they shared the same fate as her. The women decided to go in search of their children. With oil lantern in their hands, they headed to the village vigilante who joined them in the search. As they went they called out to the boys but they didn't answer. The boys couldn't hear their names because they slept off while crying. When they got to the village square, Mama Okei noticed an unusual figure lying at the foot of the udala tree. She beckoned to others to see what she had noticed. They all decided to take a look at what it was and when they did, it was their children lying helplessly on the ground. Mama Okei shouted "kweke" immediately the sharp sound woke the boys up. Seeing their mothers they burst out in tears again. They were too ashamed to tell their ordeal. The women went home with their children consoling them as they trekked back home. Seeing Kingdom all messed up Kento and his siblings chattered in mockery. Their almighty big brother was in tears. Kingdom was soaked up in his pain that he had no time for them so he allowed them to laugh to their satisfaction. He cried more because the people mocking him were the reason he went hunting in the first place. Only if they knew. His saddened and swollen face broke his mother's heart. She understood her son and his plight. His mother prepared a warm bath for him so he could clean himself up, as a mother she understood and quickly made a plan B for the family to have dinner that night. They had to soak garri as dinner. After hearing her sons story she thanked God the python did'nt hurt the children. Oh dear mother, she went to the nearest shop to get akputu bread (a strong type of small bread) for her son so he could eat before going to bed. She took her oil lantern and set out to check on the other boys to make sure they were fine too.

Morning came very fast and Kingdom remembered the injustice done to him and his friends the previous day, he thought to himself and came up with an idea. He needed to share this with his friends. He called for a meeting immediately. One thing about their friendship is they were always available when needed. Kingdom brought the idea of going back to the dreaded python's hole. Trust Akalaka he immediately opposed the idea and said count me out "ishim kamkpa" (my life is more important) Kingdom relayed his plan. The plan was to set a trap for the python, kill it and sell it to the villagers or they could extract its oil (many eke) and sell it. The flesh will be prepared as pepper soup and sold at the village square. To this, they all agreed. They decided to take the day off and embark on their journey the next day. Meeting dismissed. Kingdoms mood got better to the surprise of everybody in the neighbourhood. Oh yes, they all heard the gist many laughed and thought it served them right. Some of their peers said it served them right. They moved with poise and pride, the six were unbreakable hence the jealousy from their peers.

The day came for the operation kill the python. Akalaka sent a message through his younger sister saying he was down with fever, Moses knew he was lying and sent his sister back with a threatening message saying he would be excommunicated and never benefit from their hunt again if he didn't join them. Akalaka couldn't bear the pain of losing his friends so he joined them quickly. They were familiar with little charms so they fortified themselves against snake bites. They trod to the bush each carrying a machete. They laid the traps hoping it catches the snake. They were right the snake was in its abode and in less than 30 minutes it tried coming out to eat but it never knew what awaits it outside its hole. Just like a wind in rush the trap caught it. Immediately after went behind it and used their Machete to behead it. They couldn't carry it so they took turns to drag it all the way back home. The boys were happy things went as planned. They sold the snake and its produce. They shared the proceeds according to their age. Age was not just a number to them, it was wisdom and respect. Kingdom took the bigger as the oldest and the brain behind the plan, followed by Moses, Okei, Ofor, Jude and lastly Akalaka.

CHAPTER TWO

The journey began

Years went by and these friends grew stronger together.

Kingdom in his smartness and intelligence was admired by many in school. His English teacher took a special interest in him. He was a chronic stammerer and southpaw. His teacher decided to teach him how to write with his right hand. To Kingdom, it was almost an impossible task. He would never be able to use his right hand to write so he thought.

She devoted her time in making sure he stops writing with his left hand and promised him his right hand would be better. They began the impossible task and gradually he began to write with his right hand. But he still couldn't let go of his left hand He wrote faster with his left hand.

At some point he became ambidextrous. His friends took the new development home and the news was about him learning how to write with his right hand because he likes his teacher. (Nwata miss) as she was fondly called. His friends would laugh at him anytime they see him writing with his right hand. To him, it wasn't funny; he was doing it with love. He would go secretly to her house to help her out with her domestic chores. His friends soon. Found out, they would follow him secretly to Nwata miss's house. They would watch from afar seeing their friend smile sheepishly at everything the teacher would say. With his *wash and wear* polo and leggings, he felt cute. One day, he washed his usual leggings and polo hoping they would be dried before he gets home from school. Rain fell and drenched his clothes. He back very disappointed. He was pained. He had no other clothes he could wear so he went to his teacher's house in his school uniform.

English teacher: *"haa what happened, why are you still in your school uniform?"*

Kingdom was shy to tell her the truth so he said nothing. The teachers persuaded and he spoke up

Kingdom: *"I want to wash the dishes for you but rain drenched my clothes"*. He said amidst tears, he felt ashamed. The teacher understood perfectly what happened and how he felt.

English teacher: *"come here tomorrow at this same time"*.

Kingdom's mood became better because the teacher showed she had use for him.

Just as he was told, he came back the next day. The teacher gave him a nylon bag filled with new clothes and said

English teacher: *"take it and check if they fit"*.

Handing him the bag. Kingdom couldn't believe his eyes. The bag contained new clothes and a pair of shoes. The joy he felt knew bound. Nobody has ever been kind to him like this before. He raced to his house and showed his new gifts to his mother. His mother shouted "nwata miss emeyewoo. (teacher tried) all these for you? The next morning Kingdom was accompanied by his parents to his teacher's house. They went to thank Nwata miss for her kindness. They were poor and had suffered a whole lot so they knew how much little kindness is worth.

Apart from going hunting together with his friends, they were also known for mischief-making in the neighborhood. They killed and ate fowl they suspected had no owner. But all their mischievousness led to one thing "putting food in their stomach".

They were not religious as other people in the village were. They knew God existed but never went to church. Even their small gods "mkpidei" they never worshipped with any seriousness. They just had a little shrine in their homes because their forefathers did. Kingdom and his friends took their mischief this time around to the church.

There was a pastor who oversaw a small Pentecostal church in the village. He was well known for his evangelism and alms to the poor whenever they held their annual end of the year ingathering harvest. Kingdom gathered from a reliable source about the church and how they served sumptuous meals during their harvest Sundays. They decided to storm the church one Sunday. On that day Kingdom and his friends got dressed for church, seeing them dress for church one would think they were really going to worship not knowing they had ulterior motives. They went the church without the knowledge of their parents. They sat at the front row hoping to be the first to be served when they start sharing food. They waited all through the sermon and there was no sign of food, this got them worried and wondered if the information was wrong. Okei became furious because he had forfeited the days hunting with his father all because of church party rice. Just assured them they will get food so they decided to wait a little longer. They waited till the end of the service but there was no food. They all left in anger and blamed Jude for the wrong information. Since they couldn't any food from the church they went back to their old hobby, they go to the river to eat edible sacrifices made for the gods and goddesses.

They had no fear, some villagers had caught them earlier and had reported them to the village council members, they had been punished but they just couldn't stop. They had to survive. Berna on the hand has given her husband little or no peace since he brought home his said illegitimate daughter. She was known for always fighting her husband. Her husband Aquilla would always satisfy her with serious beatings as well. Their children grew up to know their father as the quiet man who shuts his wife up by beating her. She was really troublesome. Berna was a fierce woman and still in all her imperfections was feared by her mate. She might be poor but she doesn't take nonsense from anybody. Over the years she became well known to be troublesome that she is always engaging in fights where or whenever trouble faced her. She was short tempered. She even beat up people she owed money when they come to threaten her, she will always say "I will oaay you never goes to jail" mama Kingdom the fighter yes her daughter took after their mother, they were ready to rain brimstone one anyone who looked for their trouble. Kingdom was only brave outside, at home he was a chicken, having a warrior mother and sisters, the house was overpowered by women.

One day when they came back from school Okei brought the idea to go to the river "onoku olile" that some people came all the way from "idu" (benin) to make sacrifices with edible items. They immediately rushed down to the river. Truly there were different kinds of food. They ate tobyjeir fill and even took some chicken home. Their parents did not bother to ask them where they got the items from since they know their children were hardworking and could have gotten them as payment from their menial jobs. Each family ate the cocks that night not knowing what they had done. The next morning came, and everybody went about their various chores except for Moses. He didn't wake up. Strange..., because he wasn't sick. There was a loud cry from their compound that morning after Moses's mother tried to wake her son all to no avail. She let out a loud cry. He was an only son among five girls. The child that made her a woman. The reason she is respected in the village is the reason she is still married to her husband. Her husband had sent her packing years ago because she couldn't bear a male child. She was called barren even though she had five girls already. They called her giver because her daughters were meant for other families. Moses was born some years later after the turmoil. She was converted to a church by a catholic priest who heard her story and tried to win her soul for Christ. She conceived a few months after her conversion and gave birth to a son when the catholic priest was baptized and called Moses. Although she backslid, her husband wouldn't allow her to be a full-time Christian, he did not believe in all those Christian bullshits as he would call it.

Now where would he go from here, she knew her marriage was over. Moses's father was not left out in this pain, if only he had listened to his friends and had married a second wife, he just lost the only heir to his family name. He cried bitterly. Now he had no son. The news of Moses's death soon spread like wildfire. His friends were shocked. But he was hale and healthy last night cried his friends. Papa Moses was soon surrounded by his folks. His compound could not contain people who came to console his family. Being a true traditional man he concluded he had a problem, a serious one and he needed to consult his forefathers. He refused them to bury his son and commanded them to wait until he comes back from speaking with his ancestors. Rumors already went around the village, some said mama Moses was a witch who ate up all the male children in her womb. Some said her husband had joined a cult with his son. Some said mama Moses had gotten her son from the marine kingdom and they had collected their property back. Mama Moses heard all these and cried more. She wept uncontrollably. Meanwhile, the corpse of her son was gradually obeying nature. Papa Moses accompanied by some of his kinsmen went to the village chief priest to consult the oracle, to know what happened at night. The chief priest saw them coming and stopped them from entering his shrine. He asked who dare eat the food meant for the gods? They shouted "no one"!!! Then the chief priest told him to go home and bear his loss because he ate what was meant for the gods and he fed on yours too. Papa Moses was confused because he was sure he never tampered with what belonged to the gods, he served his ancestors truthfully. He insisted the gods were mistaken. The chief priest summoned the spirit of his dead teenage son. The spirit of his dead son appeared. Although they were afraid but his father found the courage to ask his son what happened. The dead boy replied by vomiting pieces of chicken. He needed no one to explain further he now understood everything. He cried and stormed out of the shrine. Angrily he got home and started beating his wailing wife, he poured all his anger on her. He blamed her, if only she had been an attentive mother she would have known every move of their son. If she had watched him closely and given him enough food, he wouldn't have eaten the food meant for the gods. Now papa Moses has confirmed her fears, she was surly going back home to her parents. Kingdom and his friends were summoned, they were forced to confess, they did confess and told the tale of how they ate the food meant for the gods and brought back some cocks home. The villagers were astonished by this revelation. Oh poor Moses, he had to be the scapegoat. An only son, the blind man has sight.

The parents of the boys were called and sanctioned. They were to make provision for all the items the boys ate and took home. The boys were to dance around the village naked carrying those items on their heads with native chalk all over their faces. They were to go to the river and beg for forgiveness, sleep in the shrine for four days without food, they were to return to their families on the next éké market day. These were to appease the gods. But after all these will Moses come back? No! He is gone for good. After the burial of the teenage boy as expected his mother was sent packing with her five liabilities, she called daughters.

Only if Moses will hear her mother's cry and come back to life but it was impossible. Poor woman!

Kingdom and his friends had to lay low in the meanwhile. After the atonement of their sins, they each decided to turn a new leave. Not long after they came back together again and continued their hunting and mischievous adventures but this time around they dared not go near the gods property. They decided they had an unfinished business.

CHAPTER THREE

The revelation

The pastor who always disturbed their neighborhood with his preaching was becoming a major concern to the boys.

They planned to confront him the next time he came around. As expected he came out to preach the gospel. He was ambushed and beaten by these young fellows, they warned him to stay away from their neighborhood. The pastor who believed so much in his work didn't stop his teachings. The boys would hide in their hideouts and throw stones at him. They almost killed him but it was his Cross he was ready to bear. They did this continuously until the poor preacher stopped coming to preach. One day they heard again that the preacher's church was having their annual harvest and there will be food. The boys were happy and anticipated the day. It was their harvest and the church "Souls for Christ mission " was known for its generosity during this period. They shared food and gave gifts to people who joined them in celebrating. Food was surplus and the boys ate to their fill and even took some home. During dancing, the pastor stopped seeing Kingdom and said to him "you will ride a bicycle in the house of God." Kingdom and his friends made jest of the pastor. They took off immediately they filled their bags to the brim with food. They took the food back home but this time around they explained truthfully where he got it from.

Kingdom told his mother about the vision the pastor had of him, his mother laughed and said, " tell the pastor I need a new bicycle, if he and his God wants to favor me they should buy me a new bicycle.

Years went by and they all grew up. Jude left for the city, of Asaba with his uncle to become a big trader. The rest of the boys stayed behind in the village to assist their parents in farm work

Kingdom had an aunt who everybody believed to be a witch, well she showed some characteristics a witch would possess. She was the bitter elder sister to Berna. She was always sad and wondered why she had to have just one child. She was considered the unfortunate sister, she had tried marriage many times, and each failed no one wanted to cope with such an evil woman. And they died mysteriously after they left her. Hence suspicion that she was a witch.

Kingdom never feared her. Sometimes back when Kingdom was about 10 years old. He and his friends went out for their usual Christmas stroll, where they go from house to house to ask for Christmas gifts. He convinced his friends to accompany him to his aunty's house, but they refused to follow him. The little Kingdom went alone. His aunt was surprised to see him. She welcomed him and gave him a plate of food but the smart little boy insisted on eating with his aunt. His aunty asked why and he replied and said. "You are a witch I don't want to eat alone so I would not die" the woman was shocked at his crudeness and she was sure he had heard these things from his folks. But he was right she poisoned the food. She immediately changed the plate of food and asked the little boy to join her to eat. She envied Kingdom's mother and wished she had her life, little did she know the poor woman had her fair share of failure.

Kingdom grew up to be a very fine young man. He was ready to face life and what it brings.

But does he know what is in store for him?

No! He met a lady who insisted he followed her to church. He agreed what he wouldn't do for a woman. While in church one day vision came for him again, this time around he was told he would wear a garment for God. He laughed and pished it aside. He soon became fond of going to church, he loved the way youths of his age gathered to sing, dance and pray. He became a chorister. He still wasn't a certified Christian, not to his church members until he was baptized. He tried to convert his friends too. His friends joined him except Akalaka who insisted his mother's church was better because they don't see visions there. Very funny! Although Kingdom may be a baptized member he still didn't believe in visions. One day, it was an evening service, as they were praying and singing the Holy Spirit came upon the pastor he spoke to Kingdom in a strange voice. Kingdom was terrified the things he said to Kingdom were secrets he was sure only Kingdom knew. He was facing God this time. The man of God touched him and said to him since you don't believe it better you see for yourself. Immediately Kingdom was overpowered by a strange power and he could hear and see what others could not. He saw a huge old man the man spoke to him and said "you don't believe I want you then why are you here". Kingdom replied and said"I came here because everybody goes to church so I came as well. Hhhmmm the huge old man sighed and said. You are not here by mistake, I have watched you for a very long time. When the python ate your rabbit I was there, when you and your siblings cried most night because you had nothing to eat I was there. I made food provisions the next day, didn't I? When the gods of your ancestors almost took your life for eating their food I was there. I protected you and your friends while you hunt in the deep. I made sure wild animals stayed far from you. Did you ever encounter an animal you couldn't t kill? I sent your English teacher to give you clothes when you had none to wear. All this while Kingdom stood dumbstruck, looking at the huge old man. His friends only saw a lifeless young man lying on the floor of the church. Kingdom asked the huge old man. If I work for you what do I get in return? The huge old man replied and said. : you have a lot of enemies you can't escape. Your forefathers traded you for selfish reasons. Kingdom was Still confused. He wanted to talk more but the huge old man disappeared. Immediately

Kingdom jerked back to life. He was sweating profusely amidst the overpowering discombobulating. The pastor welcomed him back with a cockish smile. The church shouted hallelujah oh yes a brother has spoken with God and he has cleared his unbelief. The typical Kingdom was quiet all through the remaining hours of the church program. His friends feared asking him anything all through the journey back home. Kingdom was silent and never spoke they were all quiet as if someone had died. Suddenly Okei burst into laughter, Ofor followed, Kingdom looking at his friend's laugh was forced to join in the laughter.They laughed uncontrollably and fell to the ground mimicking Kingdom when he fell under the anointing. Kingdom didn't find it funny this time and threatened to beat them with a stick, they ran ahead leaving him behind. He chased after them with a stick. He got home and his mother looked at him in confusion wondering how a grown-up man would soil himself like this. He looked really dirty. All thanks to the Holy Spirit. He lied to his mother he got messed up because he played football. His mother bought the lie and got off his case. He sat on his made-shift bed in deep thoughts, he still tried to believe what happened to him was real. Did he speak with God? Was that

God talking to him? He had wanted something else for himself not to become a pastor. He concluded he would forget about it. How could he preach to people? He wasn't fluent in speaking. He was a chronic stammerer, he flashed back to when the old man told him if Moses in the bible could do it then he could as well. This gave him a sleepless night. He concluded he wouldn't answer the call.

CHAPTER FOUR

The call

Few months after he left for the city of Asaba, he lived with his friend Jude. He decided to learn auto mechanics. He got registered and began his journey as an apprentice. His boss was not the loving type. He was strict but to Kingdom and his fellow apprentice, their boss was wicked, because he sometimes unnecessarily punished the boys for minor mistakes. He did it sometimes to show them how he was treated when he was an apprentice. Kingdom met other boys there too and soon made friends among them. As much as he made friends he made enemies too.

One of the good friends he made was Gregory. Gregory was a rich man child but never showed off or made anyone feel lesser than him. Their friendship was without secrets. One of the apprentices was Ike, he was filled with bitterness and never liked anybody who doesn't obey him. Most of the boys feared him so they obeyed him, he was a bully. Kingdom was a local champion so he believed he does not have to kowtow to anyone. Ike did not like the idea of sharing his territory with Kingdom. With his previous experience as an auto mechanic from Amaloye the village mechanic, he was able to learn faster than his mates. One day his boys appointed him and Ike to follow him to a construction site where they would be repairing a truck for some white men. After working Kingdom got to know one of the white men and engaged in a conversation with him. Ike watched him from afar with so much hatred. The white man urged Kingdom to drive one of the trucks. He knew his boss would not like it but he was a stubborn man. He hopped onto the truck with the white man by his side and they drove off. For a first-timer, he drove with confidence. And he drove well. The white man was impressed. Kingdom was in real trouble but he didn't mind. He was punished and he was to stay a week without wages. Gregory came to his aid. He was a friend indeed. Kingdom explored Asaba with his friend, they went to bars, restaurants, disco houses and clubs, right there Gregory showed he was rich. He spent money on drinks and girls.

They both were in for the girls. Years later Kingdom became a free man, he was no longer an apprentice. He was now a certified mechanic. Gregory left for America. This new development left Kingdom in tears because Gregory was his only true friend. He did travel from time to time to visit his family and friends. He valued respect so he learned to stay on his own. He needed to become somebody in life e took his first step by joining the choir. Although he didn't have a nice voice he loved music and played a few instruments. He learned from his father who was in a music bank back home. He played the saxophone very well. Kingdom tried recording songs a few times while he was still in the village.

He had no money to establish his auto mechanic so he joined the force. He joined the Nigerian civil defense and served for two years. One Sunday in the church, a vision came to him and he was reminded that God called him. This time the vision came in a threatening tone. He was scared and decided to stay away from church for a while. Things were not working for him as he planned. Was it his witch aunt who was after her life? Was it because he refused to work for God? Or maybe he wasn't at the right place. All these thoughts made him sad.

After a few months of job hunting, he finally got a job at a Textile mill. He got a job as a machine operator at the textile mill in Asaba. He started going to church again this time around she cared less about what the vision said to him. He was well paid so he was happy. He sent money home when necessary; he ate well and had enough to carry any woman of his choice.

His work was done by shifts so rode okada when he was free. He was making enough money for himself. After he felt the need to get married even though he knew he wasn't ready to leave the street. He joined a social-cultural association where he gets to meet people from his tribe every Sunday. Fate they say has its way of doing things. After church one day he felt reluctant to attend his usual evening meeting but something just kept pushing him to go. Finally, he went and he saw the most beautiful girl he has ever seen in his entire life. He instantly fell in love with Doris.

Although she was short but she was well endowed, her front and back where huge. Kingdom couldn't take his eyes off her. After the meeting he made enquiries about Doris and from his source he knew all he needed to know about Doris.

Kingdom allowed her to go without approaching her, he promised, next Sunday will be his day. The next Sunday came very fast, it was as if Kingdom tampered with nature to favour him. Sunday came soon with all euphoria he came to the meeting. Smiling like a fool he tried to impress Doris.

Doris was no kid so she understood what was going on anyway Kingdom was nothing close to her spec, he was short, very dark and a stammered... Kingdom pleaded with the association president who was Doris's brother-in-law to help him talk to Doris about his genuine intention. Doris heard all that was said about Kingdom, hhhmmm he seemed like a good man. But never the less she still doesn't want him. Doris lived with her sister who wants around during that time.

Her husband went to work and one day when it rained cats and dogs Doris who didn't know the compound very well on her way back from work, tried to cross a gutter fell into the gutter and twisted he ankle. It was one hell of an ordeal. It was painful. It happened that Doris and kingdom worked at the same company but never ran into each other maybe because they work different shifts. Doris was down for days without being able to walk. She was alone and in pain

Neighbours tried helping but they had work to do. Kingdom who haven't seen her around decided to visit her. He was shocked by the sight before him. Her husband's leg was swollen. He explained he had the great urge to check on her and thank God he did. He carried her to the hospital and they commenced treatment on her, behold the Kingdom she never liked was now her Knight in shining amour. He stayed with her to make sure she was okay. For a moment Kindom forgot about every other woman, he was with his heartthrob. He saw his future with Doris and everything was perfect. Right there he proposed marriage to her and she had no choice but to accept. Shortly after her recovery, she resumed work, by now they were officially an item.

Doris fell in love with this black kind man who saved her life. Doris came from a respected home so it wouldn't be a good thing if they continued seeing each other without the knowledge of their families. The marriage rites were done and her dowry was fully paid. Doris officially became Mrs Kingdom Aquilla Ogum.

Doris had to leave her church for her husband's church. A few Sundays after their marriage the holy spirit came yet again to Kingdom through an usher and said to him, this time around in a stern manner. " I am your creator and I am waiting for you, you cannot hide from me." Doris was perplexed. She had no idea what was going on. When they got home she expected an explanation from her husband but she got none. Kingdom had no intentions to explain anything to his wife. It was his burden and he chose to carry it alone. Doris was highly disappointed. For the first time, the lovey-dovey couples quarrelled seriously and slept without talking to each other. Kingdom woke up as early as 4 o'clock and left the house to histle with his Okada as usual . Doris woke up to find an empty bed. She cried. This was not the kind of love Kingdom promised her. For a new wife who was pregnant, she needed her husband not the cold shoulder.

Kingdom on his own had his own fair share of bad day. God wasn't joking or taking it lightly with his this time, he must answer thee call. The okada business was going on fine until he met a young lady, after describing her destination and accepting the cost, they drove off. If only Kingdom knew what awaited him. Few minutes into the journey Kingdom no longer felt the presence of his passenger. Out of fear he stopped bis motorcycle and looked back. Truly he was alone. How come? But he didnt stop anywahere for his passenger to come down. He turned on the ignition and suddenly there his passenger was sitting carefree behind him. In all his years as an okada man he has never experienced this. He was engulfed with fear. The lasy askes him what the problem was and he replied shakingly "nothing" she urged him to continue and so he reluctantly continued.

His trip with the mysterious lady has just started . few minutes again the lady vanished. Kingdom was now sure je was carrying a ghost. This time around he didnt stop but drove with great speed. But the lady appeared again and this time asked him not to stop or care about her disappearing. She said she had an important problem she was solving in jer kingdom. Kingdom is now more scared than ever. He begged her to go and he was no longer interested in the trip and she could keep her money. She smiled and replied "Kingdom you need the money. Your baby is coming and you need money to take care of her, you are just stubborn and your creator is angry with you, why are you refusing to work for him? Kingdom was dumbfounded and wondered how she knew his name and about his incoming baby. Now he was sure she was no ordinary being. The lady appeared and disappeared about seven more times. Finally, they got to their destination and the lady alighted and paid him. Before he zoomed off she advised him to answer his call if not he will lose all he had worked for all over the years. Months went by the vision came again and this time Kingdom responded by asking for a sign she would believe God wanted him. A sign he wanted and a sign he got. You don't give God conditions, He creates you and an do whatever He pleased you. As at dawn he set out to ride okada, this particular day would be his last as an okada rider. The night before that day was a memorable one for him, it was the naming ceremony of his precious daughter. His daughter was his mini version in a female body. He was now a proud father. He was doing well for himself. He received gifts from his colleagues and friends, it was indeed a lovely night. He toured around almost the whole city of Asaba and could get any client this was odd because passengers were never scarce in Asaba. Many hours later after burning almost all his premium motor spirit he found a passenger, a girl in her early twenties. Halfway into their journey a dog from nowhere ran into him, in his quest to avoid hitting it he somersaulted many times before he could realise what was happening his body and motorcycle were in bad condition. He tried to get up but couldn't, his legs were no longer his to control. He looked out for his passenger and the dog but couldn't find them. His body failed him and he lost consciousness. He played there for hours, no one was in sight. Doris was at home cooking when her neighbour came running with bad news, a good Samaritan had picked Kingdom from the road and taken him to the hospital. Kingdom was in a coma, Doris cried, where would she go from here, she cried more and begged God not to allow her to be a widow. Immediately she saw her husband she almost fainted, the nurses had to help her carry her baby so she wouldn't fall with her. Will her husband make it out alive? She wailed uncontrollably. She decided the church was the best place to pour her heart into God so she left for the church. God in his infinite mercy listened to her plea, her husband woke up from the coma. He woke up and immediately requested to see his pastor. He begged his pastor to help him secure the next available form for pastoral school. Surprisingly Kingdoms wounds and broken bones got healed like nothing happened. His wife was surprisedat his outburst, he told his pastor he was ready ro answer Gods call. His eyes has seen shege. He had gone to hell and back. He had no choice but to ride that bicycle for God. Kingdom was discharged few days later and like he earlier wished , he got admitted into pastoral school. His wife and child had to relocate to the village to wait for him for two years. While waiting for her hubby Doris opened a bukar in the village, she sold food early in the morning to students and farmers who left home early. Her husband was a student and she had to survive with her child. Two years later Kingdom graduated and was deployed to his first church in the deep thick of umuahia village. He preached and won souls for God. He was transferred again to another small church with no members. He had to start from scratch. His ministry was all about going to poor places to win souls for God. Deep villages where he won the souls of just old people and sometimes a few youths. The church forbade side hustle so this was a problem for him. He is no longer a father of one but many now. How would he take care of his growing family?

CHAPTER SIX

Dissatisfied

Was this his calling or it wasn't just his time? He was only transferred to poor places, the thickest bushes, and undeveloped villages. In most of these villages, he engaged in farming but this was not what he wanted for himself, this was not how he envisioned his ministry. The church wanted it to be so. If only they could transfer him to towns where his children could get a better education and a better life. This continued for years and it disturbed him greatly, he did his best and preached the gospel. His mates were making money, building houses and taking care of bigger responsibilities. All he had was for his immediate family alone and sometimes was never sufficient. Why was he suffering? Did he do anything wrong? Was this what God promised him? Doris the patient wife became tired. At each national church conference, she sees her mate and most of them mock her and tell her she and her husband were behind because they didn't know the way. She will always ask, "what is the way" although she agreed to embark on this journey with her husband but not on an empty stomach. They had suffered, they were never transferred to a buoyant church where they would work less and enjoy.   Maybe The bushes were his calling. His friends convinced him to follow their way he knew their way wasn't clear but he decided to hear them out this time. Maybe God has forsaken you and He is no longer with you just follow us to the mountains they told him. Kingdom no longer cared if God answered him or not he just wanted to eradicate poverty from his lineage. He followed his friends to the mountains but what life they say isn't fair. At the mountain, they met a native doctor, Kingdom relayed his predicament to him and the native doctor said to him "your problem is simple you have wealth but you are still far from it. The gods of your forefathers are solidly behind you and no death planned by humans and spirits can kill you. In exchange, they delayed your wealth because you will misuse it and be filled with pride and you will die ever before you learn your lessons. He was shocked because deep down he thought he was a humble man. Well, money they say brings out the real you. A man is not considered humble until he touches wealth. The native doctor said again, all these can be tampered with if you are man enough to override your chi. (destiny) you will have to sacrifice someone from your household, someone you love very much, your wife or any of your children. Kingdom who has received a great amount of loss, couldn't bear to lose another child, his wife would run mad. His wife was not an option too. He lost his mother a few years before, then, it was a heavy blow to him. After all these thoughts, he came to his senses and wondered why he was there in the first place, he will continue praying to God and one day God would answer him. He made up his mind to go back home, he told the native doctor he could never touch his family for anything and his ancestors can continue protecting him with all he cares, God was his real protector. His friends were disappointed and they mocked him and called him a failure, he was a failure to them but to God, he was a success. He trusted God. Kingdom got home, for one whole week he spent the better part of his time in the church. What he do without God. He watched his friends build houses, open new churches, bought cars and some were transferred to big churches but he remained steadfast in prayer, he felt bad that God hasn't answered him but God was faithful in some ways, many times he contemplated leaving the church for another church, he always had a warning in his dreams.

He obeyed God and served him truly with all he had, so what went wrong. Where did he go wrong?

It was 25 years already and he was still waiting on God. He never hurt anyone intentionally and he apologised anytime he offended anyone, he visited his members, he was humble and kind, he cared for the needy with the little he had why was he suffering. One day something came to his mind, was it the sacrifices he ate when he was still a kid? If that was the case his friends were all doing well why him.? He needed to break the yoke of poverty. He engaged himself in farming and his wife started a petite trade to support the family. His first daughter was now grown and had left home to look for green pastures. He was ashamed and scared of what his daughter would become trying to break the yoke of poverty. Asking God to protect her was all he could do. Will God hear this one? When will his time come, he was gradually ageing and becoming feeble, what God had planned to do later let Him do it fast, because if he dies a sad man he will never be happy with God.